MW01087344

Kingdom of Wisteria

Written by Eva Rice and Freda Roberts
Illustrated by Andrieanna Barnes

ISBN 978-1-936352-70-8
1-936352-70-2

© 2010 Eva Rice and Freda Roberts
All rights reserved

No part of this publication may be reproduced in any form or stored, transmitted or recorded by any means without the written permission of the author.

Published by Mirror Publishing
Milwaukee, WI 53214

Printed in the USA.

To children everywhere that love to read
and be read to

Flowers of every color draped the landscape in the Kingdom of Wisteria, but the magnificent purple wisteria was the most abundant.

The rivers carved their paths and stretched across the lush kingdom creating lakes and streams. Beautiful cascading waterfalls formed ponds of crystal clear blue water. It was a paradise on earth, except…Amber grabbed Laurel's hair.

"Give me back my brush!" she screamed. "I didn't take it. Stop accusing me of things." Laurel shoved Amber and watched her fall backward into the pond.

"Laurel, cut it out," yelled Lilly. "You shouldn't shove anyone!" Lilly stretched her arm toward Amber and helped her out of the water. "Oh, stay out of it, Lilly," reprimanded Brie. "Amber is always accusing one of us of something. She deserves to be pushed."

The girls played and swam in the pond closest to the castle everyday, but, as usual, their play turned into fights.

The girls bickered all the way back to the castle which sat atop the tallest mountain in the kingdom.

"Wait until I tell Father you pushed me," whined Amber. Brie shot Amber a stern look. "You're such a baby. Stop causing trouble." Amber brought her arm back, ready to throw it full-force at Brie.

"GIRLS!" King Drake grabbed Amber's hand. "You are princesses, not warriors. Come to the throne room right now!" The four sisters, still bickering under their breath, followed their father to his throne.

King Drake sat in his majestic chair. The girls stood impatiently before him. A father, not a king, glared at his daughters. I've never seen him this upset, thought Lilly.

"Your constant bickering gives me no rest and disrupts my kingdom. I am dividing Wisteria into five kingdoms, and each of you will have your own.

But, be aware, each kingdom will have only one feature. You must live without your sisters and what they possess on their land…FOREVER. It is decreed!"

Lilly watched as Laurel, Brie, and Amber giggled and hurried off to take control of their own kingdoms. "Where are you going? What about your belongings?" she asked. Brie turned to Lilly. "We'll come back for our things!" Lilly stayed behind. Four separate kingdoms?

Her father rose from his chair to leave. "Father, please tell me what each kingdom will have. I'm not sure if this is a good idea."

"Lilly, I didn't think you would just run off without giving this some thought. Your land will have bountiful lakes, streams, and rivers. But, there will be no animals, and no vegetation or trees."

"As far as your sisters' kingdoms, Amber will have every kind of vegetation imaginable, but that is all. There will be no trees, no animals, and no water. Laurel will have every variety of animal, but that is all.

There will be no vegetation, trees, or water. Brie will have lush forests, filled with trees of every kind, but that is all. Her land will not have any vegetation, animals, or water."

"But, Father, each kingdom will not survive without the other. Although I will have water and fish, without trees there will be no shade from the hot summer sun.

I will need a variety of foods to eat, but I will not have any meat or vegetables. And, no beautiful flowers to look at."

Lilly's eyes roamed around the throne room. "And…and, my sisters' kingdoms will become ruined without water. Oh, no!" Lilly raced out of the throne room and into the courtyard.

"BRIE! AMBER! LAUREL! WAIT!" Her sisters were sitting in their carriages, ready to go off to their kingdoms. "What's the matter, Lilly?" shouted Laurel.

Brie and Amber jumped out of their carriages. "What's wrong?" they asked. "You cannot leave," said Lilly.

"We cannot live without each other." "Oh, Lilly, you're being silly, as usual," said Amber as she walked back toward her carriage, kicking the dirt on her way. "I want my own kingdom!"

"Amber's right," said Brie. "All we do is fight. It will be a pleasure to be away from each other." Brie stepped back into her carriage and closed the door.

Lilly lowered her head and fell to her knees. Tears began to fall down her cheeks. "How do I stop them?" she whispered.

Suddenly, Lilly felt a hand on her shoulder. "Why are you so upset?" asked Laurel. "We will see each other now and then."

Lilly lifted her head. "You don't understand. We will never see each other again. I will have the only kingdom with water. Amber will have vegetation, Brie will have trees, and you will have animals. We will each only have one resource on our land. Your kingdoms will perish without water."

Laurel took hold of Lilly's arm and helped her up. "Oh!" she cried. "You're right. This is terrible! We didn't really listen to father. BRIE! AMBER! Get over here right now!"

Yelling and jumping up and down, Laurel got the girls' attention. She motioned for them to come. Lilly wiped her tears and felt a smile spread across her face even though Brie and Amber gave her an annoyed look.

"This better be good," said Amber as she and Brie walked to their sisters. They huddled together in the courtyard, and Lilly explained what their father intended to do.

The girls trembled as they thought of what might have happened if they had gone off to their own kingdoms.

Amber grabbed Lilly and kissed her cheek. "Thank you, Lilly, for thinking things through. I'm sorry for always causing trouble. We are sisters. We are forever."

The sisters hugged. Then, they went to find their father to tell him that they didn't want their own kingdoms.

Still thinking matters over while searching the castle for her father, Lilly let out a little giggle…. father wouldn't have really done that.

The End

CPSIA information can be obtained
at www.ICGtesting.com
Printed in the USA
LVIC091133141012
302763LV00003B

9781936352708